The Secret Lives of Animals

The Secret Lives of Gorillas

by Julia Barnes

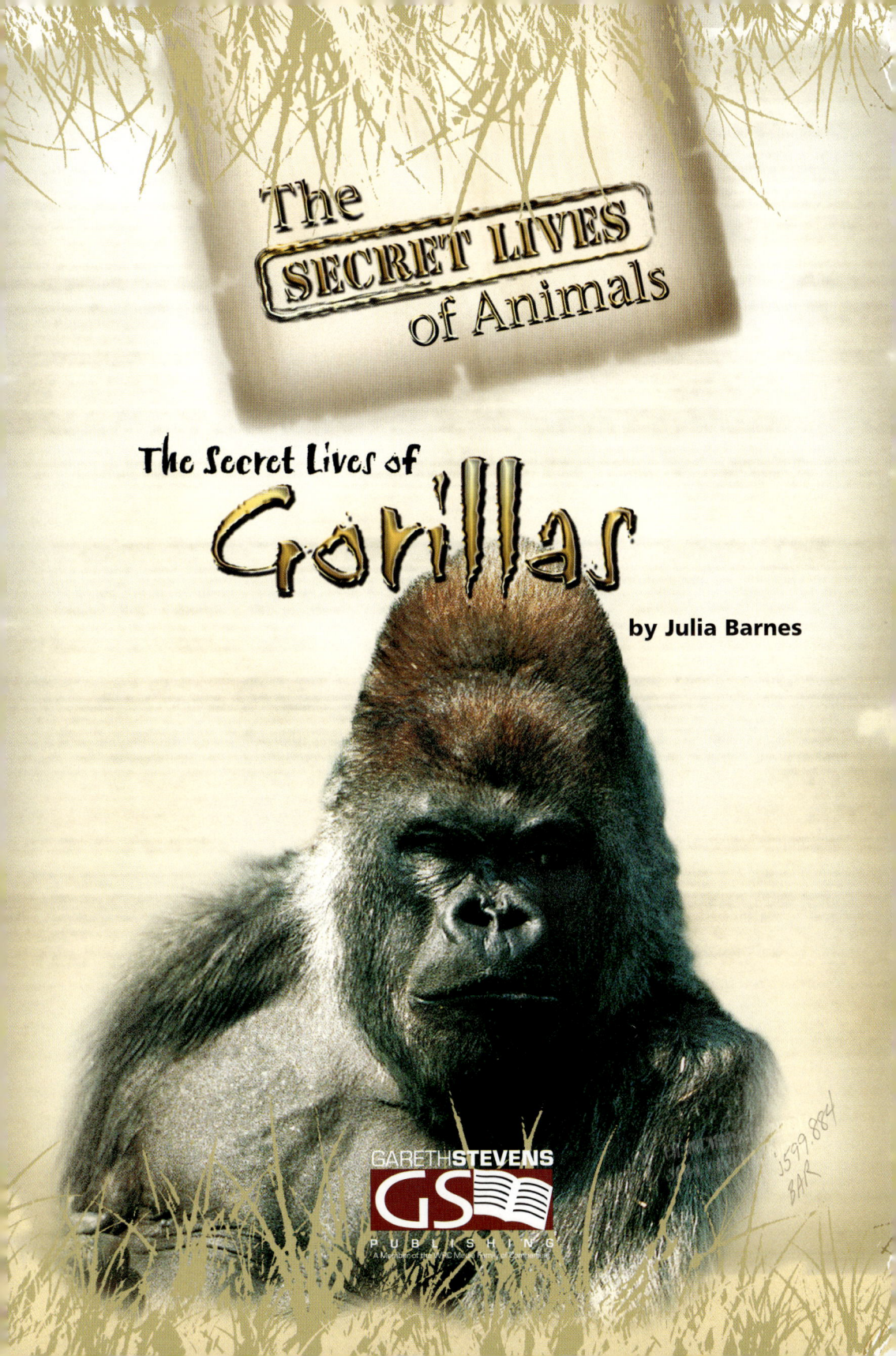

Please visit our web site at: www.garethstevens.com
For a free color catalog describing Gareth Stevens Publishing's list of high-quality
books and multimedia programs, call 1-800-542-2595 (USA) or 1-800-387-3178 (Canada).
Gareth Stevens Publishing's fax: (414) 332-3567.

Library of Congress Cataloging-in-Publication Data

Barnes, Julia, 1955-
　The secret lives of gorillas / Julia Barnes.
　　p. cm. — (The secret lives of animals)
　Includes bibliographical references and index.
　ISBN-13: 978-0-8368-7658-1 (lib. bdg.)
　1. Gorilla—Juvenile literature.　I. Title.
　QL737.P96B35　2007
　599.884—dc22　　　　　　　　　2006035327

This North American edition first published in 2007 by
Gareth Stevens Publishing
A Member of the WRC Media Family of Companies
330 West Olive Street, Suite 100
Milwaukee, WI 53212 USA

This edition copyright © 2007 by Gareth Stevens, Inc.
Original edition copyright © 2006 by Westline Publishing.
Additional end matter copyright © 2007 by Gareth Stevens, Inc.

Gareth Stevens editor: Gini Holland
Gareth Stevens designer: Kami M. Strunsee
Gareth Stevens art direction: Tammy West
Gareth Stevens production: Jessica Yanke and Robert Kraus

Photo credits: copyright © istockphoto.com: Bill Kennedy front cover, p. 24;
Rick Rhay p. 4; Peter Chen p. 6; Bill Kennedy p. 8; Tauno Novek p. 11; kevdog818 p. 12;
Steven Tilston p. 13; Rob Friedman p. 14; Stefan Klein p. 16; Stefan Klein p. 18; Udo Weber p. 21;
Michael Shake p. 22; Craig Jones p. 25; zennie p. 26; Bobbie Osborne p. 27; Pete Collins p. 28 ;
Wolfgang Moeller p. 29; copyright© Oxford Scientific Films: Stan Osolinski pp. 17, 20;
Andrew Plumptre p. 23. All other images copyright © Westline Publishing Limited.

All rights reserved. No part of this book may be reproduced, stored in a retrieval system,
or transmitted in any form or by any means, electronic, mechanical, photocopying,
recording, or otherwise, without the prior written permission of the copyright holder.

Printed in the United States of America

1 2 3 4 5 6 7 8 9 10 10 09 08 07 06

Contents

INTRODUCING THE GORILLA	4
THE WAYS OF GORILLAS	6
THE GORILLA'S PERFECT BODY	8
HOW A GORILLA SEES THE WORLD	10
DISCOVERING SPECIAL SKILLS	12
WHAT DOES A GORILLA DO ALL DAY?	14
HOW DO GORILLAS COMMUNICATE?	16
TIMES OF TROUBLE	20
WHEN GORILLAS ARE READY TO BREED	22
THE FAMILY LIFE OF GORILLAS	24
THE YOUNG GORILLAS GROW UP	26
GORILLAS AND PEOPLE	28
GLOSSARY	30
MORE BOOKS TO READ/WEB SITES	31
INDEX	32

Introducing the Gorilla

The gorilla is the largest ape in the world. Along with the chimpanzee, it is our closest relative in the animal kingdom. The powerful gorilla rarely uses its strength to fight. It is a peace-loving **vegetarian** that lives within a close-knit family group. What is life really like for a gorilla? What are a gorilla's favorite pastimes? What happens when two gorillas fight? To find out, we need to enter the secret world of gorillas.

SECRETS OF SUCCESS

The gorilla lives in tropical African rain forests, where the climate is hot and wet. The temperature is about 80 degrees Fahrenheit (26° Celsius) all year, and the rain forests may get up to 8 feet (2.5 meters) of rainfall each year. Some gorillas live in low-lying forests or swampland at sea level. Others make their homes on mountain slopes at altitudes of 10,000 feet (3,050 m). Gorillas only occupy a small amount of land.

While it can be very gentle, the gorilla is one of the most powerful of all animals.

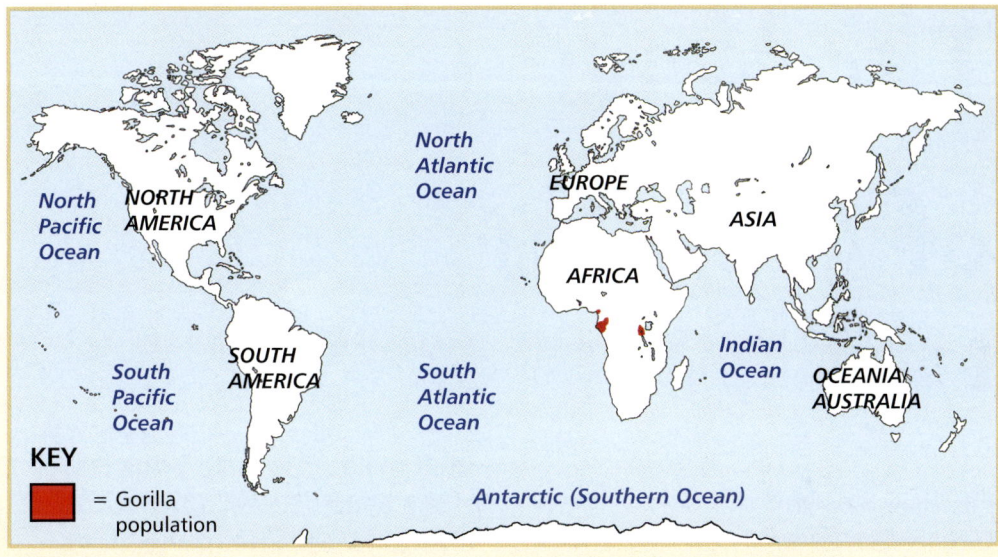

The gorilla lives only in a few areas of Africa, where it is very warm and damp.

How have they managed to survive in the wild?
- The gorilla can find everything it needs within a tropical rain forest.
- Gorillas live in groups, protected by powerful male gorillas.
- Gorillas are not normally **aggressive** unless threatened.
- The gorilla has no natural enemies in the wild.

WHERE DO GORILLAS LIVE?

Two **species** of gorillas exist. The western gorilla lives in west central Africa — in countries including the Central African Republic, Gabon, the Republic of the Congo, the Democratic Republic of Congo, Cameroon, and Equatorial Guinea.

The eastern gorilla lives in East Africa — in countries including the Democratic Republic of Congo, Rwanda, and Uganda.

Western gorillas are divided between lowland gorillas and Cross River gorillas. Eastern gorillas are divided between lowland and mountain gorillas. All four types look alike and have similar ways of life, although they are separted from one another.

About ten million years ago, in the Miocene epoch, a huge lake in the Congo basin separated the two gorilla populations. When the lake dried out, the gorillas stayed in their separate homes in the east and the west.

The Ways of Gorillas

Like all animals living in the wild, gorillas need a few essential things to survive.

FINDING A HOME
Gorillas live in family groups, which are known as **bands**. Up to forty animals may live in a band, but usually, bands have between five and ten members. A typical band will include three adult females, four or five young male and female gorillas of different ages, and one adult male. The male is the leader of the band. He is known as the **silverback** because of the silvery-white hair on his back.

The band has a home base in the forest. The **home range** that it occupies is small, measuring between 2 and 12 square

The big, male silverback (*left*) is the protector of his band, and he is also the band's decision maker.

Gorillas need to eat large quantities of food every day.

miles (5 and 30 square kilometers). Because the gorilla is such a large animal, it needs to spend much of the day eating. It cannot waste time traveling around a large territory. A gorilla band does not attempt to defend its territory, and so a number of territories will overlap. This overlap of territories does not cause problems between the different gorilla bands.

FOOD

It is amazing to think that an animal as large and powerful as a gorilla lives only on fruit and other plants. They may sometimes eat insects, but they are otherwise vegetarian. Gorillas eat vines, wild celery, thistles, leaves, bamboo shoots, and some tree bark. In the lush rain forests of West Africa, there are many fruit trees, and western gorillas will go in search of fruit when it is ripe. The eastern gorilla has less fruit available for its diet, and so it has to eat leaves and other parts of plants. Plants and fruits have a lot of moisture, so the gorilla does not have to search for fresh drinking water very often.

A BREEDING PARTNER

All animals living in the wild have a strong desire to breed and produce young, because this is the only way that a species will survive for future generations. To breed regularly, a silverback will gather a **harem** of females. If another male attempts to steal his females, there will be a fight, which could end in the death of one of the male gorillas.

The Gorilla's Perfect Body

The gorilla is one of the biggest and most powerful animals that live in tropical rain forests. Because they are big and powerful, they can live without fear of other animals in the rain forest.

SIZE

The male gorilla has another reason for needing a large body. The bigger and more powerful a male gorilla is, the more chance he has of establishing his own family group. The silverback must attract females and also protect the group. For this reason, male and female gorillas are very different in size. A male is twice the size of a female. A **mature** silverback weighs about 397 pounds (180 kilograms) compared to a female, which weighs about 198 pounds (90 kg). A male is also taller, measuring about 5 feet 6 inches (1.7 m), while a female is about 4 feet 6 inches (1.4 m) in height. Both males and females have stocky builds with longer arms than legs.

A silverback looks so impressive that he can usually scare away rivals without needing to fight.

Gorillas use a style of walking known as **knuckle walking**. They move on all fours, using the soles of their feet, but not the palms of their hands. Instead, they curl their fingers into their hands, putting weight on the knuckles.

A gorilla can stand upright when it wants to reach for something, and a male will usually stand on his hind legs when he is **threatening** another gorilla so that he looks as big and ferocious as possible.

The head of a silverback gorilla is massive, with a great, bulging forehead.

HEAD

You can also see the difference between male and female gorillas when you look at the size of their heads. The male's head is much bigger, with a huge, bulging forehead. He also has a large, bony crest on the top of his head, which is used to support the muscles he needs to work his powerful jaw. Both males and females need large **molar teeth** to chew and grind the plants they eat. Because the male is so much bigger and needs more food, his teeth are larger and his jaw muscles are more powerful.

The male also has much bigger **canine teeth**, which he uses for tearing food and for fighting.

HANDS AND FEET

The gorilla's hands and feet look very much like ours. We are better at using our hands than gorillas are. The gorilla, however, can grip equally well with both its hands and its feet! Gripping with all four limbs is very useful when a gorilla is finding and preparing its food.

How a Gorilla Sees the World

Imagine yourself inside a gorilla's body. How does it feel to be the biggest **primate** in the world?

THE PRIMATE FAMILY
The gorilla is a member of the primate order, which includes monkeys, apes, and human beings.

When you look at a gorilla, you can see that its features are similar to other primates, such as humans.

Obviously, gorillas and humans have developed in different ways, but the gorilla and the chimpanzee are humans' closest relatives in the animal kingdom. Both these animals see the world very much as we do.

EYESIGHT
The gorilla has small, dark brown eyes in the front of its face, allowing it to see in front and to the sides. In some ways, the gorilla sees as well as we do, but it is near-sighted. This means that a gorilla will hold an object close to its eyes for inspection because it is not very good at seeing things that are far away. The gorilla can see in color, which is useful for spotting fruit when it is ripe.

HEARING
The gorilla has tiny ears that lie close to the skull, but they are very effective, giving the

Gorillas use their sense of touch when they are finding food and investigating different objects.

gorilla excellent hearing. The sense of hearing is very important for animals that live in rain forests. They often cannot see each other because of the dense **vegetation** in the rain forests. Gorillas use their hearing to keep track of band members and also to sense danger.

SMELL
The gorilla has a good sense of smell, although it is not as highly developed as it is in animals that hunt other animals for their food. The gorilla uses its nose to smell whether or not food is fresh and also to find out if any animals have been visiting its territory. A gorilla is able to pick up the scent of a gorilla that is not part of its band. Scientists have also discovered that gorillas recognize the smell of human sweat.

The gorilla has its own unique noseprint, which is like our fingerprints. No two gorilla noseprints are alike, so their noseprints can help scientists identify individual gorillas.

TOUCH
Like people, gorillas have a highly developed sense of touch, which they use for feeling, gripping, and manipulating objects.

TASTE
Mountain gorillas have more leaves in their diet than lowland gorillas do. The leaves they find to eat are often very bitter tasting. Western lowland gorillas eat fruit when it is in season, and, like people, they seem to have favorite foods. They consider figs, which are sweet tasting, a great treat.

Discovering Special Skills

Gorillas are rated as the most intelligent land animal, after humans. We are still finding out how gorillas use their brainpower. Scientists have carried out tests on gorillas in zoos and have been amazed by the results. One gorilla has been taught more than one hundred words in sign language and has learned how to use a series of signs to form a short sentence. More importantly, a few gorillas in captivity have shown that they will use sign language to get things that they need. Using language with a purpose is more intelligent than, for example, parrots that speak words but do not use them with meaning. How do gorillas use their great intelligence in the wild?

SOCIAL BONDS

Gorillas stand out in the animal kingdom because of the way they live their lives in highly developed social groups. Their ability to organize in groups shows their intelligence and makes them similar to people. Like people, gorillas form close relationships with each other.

A family group will live together in complete peace for many years,

An adult gorilla has a good memory and knows all the best places to find food and nesting material.

accepting the decisions made by the silverback.

The silverback protects and cares for all members of his group. He acts lovingly and playfully with his children, and he will even look after a young gorilla that has lost its mother. Adult females accept the silverback's protection. They devote their time to caring for their offspring.

USING TOOLS

Scientists see the ability to make and use tools as a sign of an animal's brainpower. Chimpanzees have often been seen using tools in the wild, such as when they select long sticks to fish out termites from nests. It is only recently, however, that we have seen gorillas using tools. A gorilla was spotted using a walking stick to test the depth of water in a stream that it was trying to cross. On another occasion, a female gorilla used a tree trunk as a bridge when she wanted to get across a stretch of water.

Gorillas are also very skilled at **foraging** for food and then preparing it. A gorilla has been seen wrapping leaves around prickly thistles before eating them, and mountain gorillas strip the outer layer from wild celery to get to the juicy plant inside.

The members of this band of mountain gorillas eat, sleep, and travel together.

What Does a Gorilla Do All Day?

Gorillas are shy, secretive animals that like to keep themselves well hidden in the wild. Scientists have had problems studying western gorillas because they often disappear deep into the rain forest. Tracking eastern gorillas, which live on forest edges and mountainsides with less natural **cover**, has been easier.

EARLY MORNING

A band of gorillas will wake up soon after sunrise and start searching for food. Because gorillas are so large and their food is not high in **nutrients**, they must eat vast amounts every day. An adult male needs to eat 40 pounds (18 kg) of food every day!

Gorillas spend most of their time foraging for food on the ground, but young gorillas, which do not weigh as much, climb trees to find fruit to eat.

MIDDAY REST

The silverback decides when it is time to find a place to rest. The band gathers around the silverback, and they will settle down for a couple of hours. The younger gorillas take the opportunity to play. The adults groom themselves

Gorillas spend a lot of time grooming themselves, and they will also groom other members of the band.

14

The silverback decides when its band should go in search of fresh food.

to keep their coats free from dirt and **parasites**. Gorillas also groom each other as one way of forming close ties with other band members. Mothers groom their offspring, and a female may have the honor of grooming the chief silverback. The adult females that are not related do not groom each other.

AFTERNOON

In the afternoon, the silverback gets the band together, and they will begin searching for food again. The band travels less than one mile (1.5 km) a day. The silverback decides when it is time to move on, which is usually when an area has been eaten down. The silverback then leads his group to another good feeding place. He has detailed knowledge of the home range, which he uses to help feed his family. He knows where the best fruit trees are located and when the fruit will be ready for picking.

BEDTIME

At dusk, the silverback calls the band together, and they settle for the night. Each gorilla builds a nest out of leaves and branches, placing it either on the ground or in a tree. Mothers and babies share a nest, but the rest of the band members have their own individual nests. Every night, the gorillas find a new place to build their nests. This practice ensures that they all have clean beds every night, which helps prevent disease in the band.

15

How Do Gorillas Communicate?

Gorillas have a close understanding of each other, and they communicate by using different facial expressions and by using a variety of sounds.

EXPRESSIONS

As with people, every gorilla has a different face. When scientists study gorillas in the wild, they take close-up photos of all the band members, so they can recognize each gorilla. If you look at a gorilla's face, it is easy to imagine what the gorilla is feeling because it makes expressions that are very like our own. Some of their expressions have meanings that are different from ours. Here are some faces gorillas make:
- A gorilla has a play face when it is bright-eyed and alert.
- If a gorilla keeps folding its lips, it is feeling tense.

Each gorilla looks different and uses different expressions to show its feelings.

- When a gorilla is trying to figure something out, it may stick its tongue out of its mouth.
- A gorilla that keeps on yawning is probably feeling stressed.

VOICES

Gorillas need to communicate by sound because, when they are feeding or traveling, they may become separated from one another among the trees and plants of the rain forest. Gorillas make fifteen distinct sounds, and each one means something different. They include the following:

- Whines and cries are made by infant gorillas when they are unhappy or uncomfortable.
- Chuckles are often heard when young gorillas are playing.
- Deep belches, which are a sign of contentment, are heard among feeding gorillas.
- Pig-like grunts are used to settle squabbles or to establish a right of way when gorillas are feeding close together. Adult gorillas will discipline youngsters with grunts.
- Low growls are a sign of pleasure and contentment.
- Hoots are a warning sign to alert band members to danger.

- Male gorillas roar and growl when they are threatening each other.
- An ear-splitting scream may be used to drive off a **rival** gorilla.

THREAT DISPLAY

Gorillas do not defend their ranges, but a silverback is always alert in case another male tries to get to the females of his band. The silverback needs to show his

A gorilla hoots to warn other band members of danger.

17

This angry silverback, who is warning another gorilla to keep away, gives his rival a hard stare.

strength and power, but he will try to avoid a fight. The silverback, therefore, puts on a threat display, which he hopes will drive away the rival gorilla. While the silverback is putting on his display, the females and youngsters in his band have the chance to retreat to the safety of the forest.

A threat display follows a nine-step pattern, with the silverback becoming more **aggressive** as the display goes on.

The nine steps of the silverback's threat display are:
1. The silverback makes a hooting sound, which starts slowly and then gets faster.
2. He grabs some leaves and stuffs them into his mouth.
3. The silverback rises onto two legs.
4. He throws vegetation at the rival gorilla.
5. The silverback beats his chest with cupped hands. He stands at full height and shows off his powerful body to frighten off the rival gorilla.
6. Still standing, the silverback will kick out with one leg.
7. He will then run sideways toward the rival gorilla.
8. The silverback tears up vegetation and beats it on the ground.
9. He ends the display by thumping on the ground with the palms of his hands.

Other aggressive silverback behavior includes fierce stares at the rival, head jerks, and sudden lunges.

The two gorillas may roar and growl at each other, and occasionally, a gorilla will scream. Throughout the display, the two gorillas make no physical contact with one another. In most cases, one silverback will drive off its rival without either animal becoming physically harmed.

The silverback will put on an aggressive display to scare away rival males.

Times of Trouble

If animals as large and powerful as silverbacks fight, the results can be disastrous. Gorillas try to avoid fights as much as possible.

FIGHTING GORILLAS
A young silverback's greatest goal is to establish his own harem of females. His best chance of success is to take over an existing band. Taking over a band is very difficult if that band has a strong and fit silverback. A silverback at the height of his powers can protect his females with threat displays and drive off the rival. If the silverback is old and losing his powers, however, the young silverback may stand his ground and fight.

If an old silverback is faced with a much stronger rival, he may give up the struggle. The old silverback will then walk away in defeat, leaving his band forever. He will spend the rest of his life living alone.

If the two silverbacks are evenly matched, the fight is vicious, with both animals

A silverback beats his chest to show off his strength and power.

20

using their incredible strength and their ferocious canine teeth to inflict terrible injuries. The fight only ends when one of the animals is killed.

OLD AGE

In the wild, a gorilla lives to be about thirty-five years old. In a zoo, gorillas can live for fifty years or more because they do not have to find their own food or compete with rival male gorillas.

Disease is a major cause of death among gorillas in the wild, and a large number of gorillas die from pneumonia (a lung infection).

When a female gorilla becomes old, she manages fairly well. The silverback protects her, and, as the band does not travel long distances, she can still keep up with them.

Life is much harder for an old silverback that cannot hold onto his own band. He may be killed by a rival, or, if he is driven away, he faces a **solitary** life, without the help and support of other band members. He no longer has any females to groom him or keep him company. At the same time, because he has no natural enemies — aside from humans — he may get along fairly well on his own, alone in the rain forest.

As a silverback grows old, he risks losing his females to a younger male.

When Gorillas Are Ready to Breed

When a silverback is about twelve years old, he is ready to breed with females. He may have to wait a few years, however, before he can establish his own harem of females. A young silverback may take over an existing band, or he may attract a lone female and start up his own band. In large bands, where more than twenty gorillas live together, the silverback may allow another male to breed with some of the females, but he will make sure that he always has first choice.

CHILD KILLERS

If a silverback takes over a band, he will want to breed with the females as soon as possible. When a female is rearing a baby, she is not ready for breeding. The silverback will therefore kill an infant gorilla so that its mother will breed with him. About

A silverback will not try to establish his own band until he is fully mature.

The silverback (*right*) that is largest will get first choice of the females when they are ready to breed. The silverback is always much larger than the female gorillas.

one-third of all gorilla infants are killed by male gorillas.

SEACHING FOR A SILVERBACK
A female gorilla is ready for breeding when she is about ten years of age. If she lives in a big band where there is more than one silverback, she may decide to stay in the band she was born in. In a large band with more than one silverback, she has a chance to breed with a male that is not her father. Most females move out and search for a silverback that will be a breeding partner and a protector.

A female may not have to travel very far to find what she wants. A silverback with his own band may live only a short distance away, or she may find a lone silverback that is trying to set up his own band.

The female makes her choice depending on the power and strength of the silverbacks that she finds. She will look for a male that she thinks will be able to protect her. She may also decide to join a silverback if his home range has good supplies of food.

23

The Family Life of Gorillas

A female gorilla is pregnant for eight to nine months. She usually gives birth to a single baby that weighs between 4 and 5 pounds (1.8 and 2.3 kg).

Gorilla twins are very rare. If twins are born, one of the babies will usually die because the mother gorilla cannot manage to carry and feed two infants. Usually, the smaller of the twins will not survive.

EARLY DAYS

A baby gorilla can see and hear as soon as it is born, and it has a fine covering of hair. For the first weeks, the newborn baby is completely dependent on its mother. The mother holds her baby close to her belly. The baby gorilla spends its time drinking milk from the mother and sleeping.

Within a few weeks, the baby is able to grip onto the hairs of

Gorillas are patient and devoted mothers.

its mother's belly. Once it is able to hang on to its mother in this way, the mother can move around more easily and forage for food. She can also keep pace with the band when it is traveling to a new feeding area.

When the baby gorilla is about nine weeks old, it starts to crawl. The mother keeps a very close eye on her baby and makes sure it does not stray too far away. When the baby is sixteen weeks old, it starts to ride on its mother back when the band is on the move. A young gorilla is able to follow the band on foot by the time it is eighteen months old, but most prefer the safety of riding on their mothers' backs and continue to take piggyback rides until they are more than three years old.

The silverback cares for and protects the infants in his band.

IN THE BAND

A baby gorilla is loved and cared for by all members of the band. To begin with, the baby stays very close to its mother, but by the time it is walking, at about thirty-five weeks, it will mix with the other gorillas. The silverback is a patient father and will allow a young gorilla to climb all over him when he is resting in the middle of the day.

A baby gorilla develops twice as fast as a human baby, but it keeps feeding from its mother for longer. A gorilla will take milk from its mother until it is about three years of age.

The Young Gorillas Grow Up

A baby gorilla grows up surrounded by caring adults and is looked after by its mother until it is nearly six years old. In spite of all this support, many baby gorillas fail to survive. Young gorillas are hunted by leopards, killed by male gorillas, or they may die from disease. About forty percent of gorillas will die before they are six years old.

SURVIVAL SKILLS

As a young gorilla grows up, it must learn the skills that it needs to survive in the wild. A gorilla learns by watching and copying other gorillas. A young gorilla sees how its mother and other members of the band forage for

As a young gorilla grows up, it becomes skilled at finding its own food.

food. The gorilla finds out what is good to eat and will remember where favorite foods can be found. From about four years of age, a young gorilla will nest on its own. The youngster learns how to build a nest by watching its mother.

The gorillas also learn through play. Every band has young gorillas of different ages, and the youngsters play all sorts of games together. Some of the games, such as chasing each other and playing "follow the leader," are just the same as those played on the playgrounds of young people. The young males also wrestle and play-fight, preparing for the time when they will need to defend a band of their own.

Young gorillas must also learn the social skills that are needed to live in a group. By watching how the adults behave, and being scolded if they are naughty, the youngsters learn how to be good members of the gorilla community.

MOVING ON

A silverback drives young males away from his band when they are grown up and ready to start

The youngsters must learn their place within the gorilla band.

breeding. He does not want them competing with him. Sometimes, a few males get together and form a **bachelor band** until they are ready to form their own groups. Females who have found a mate give birth every four years. Because so many infants die before they can reach adulthood, it takes a very long time for the gorilla population to grow.

Gorillas and People

The gorilla is one of our closest relatives in the animal kingdom, after chimpanzees. In some ways, we find it easy to understand the feelings of this magnificent animal. This is a creature that can even use sign language, in a simple form, in the same way that people do.

The gorilla wants nothing more than to live its life in the privacy of the rain forest. Unfortunately, people have not allowed the gorilla to remain undisturbed. People have changed the world so much that the gorilla is now struggling to survive in the wild.

THREATS TO SURVIVAL

Gorillas have no natural enemies in the wild, but numbers have fallen so dramatically that they are now close to **extinction**. Only 50,000 gorillas remain in Africa — the only place in the world where they live. Most of these are western lowland gorillas. Only 2,500 eastern lowland gorillas, as few as 600 mountain gorillas, and under 300 Cross River gorillas now survive.

Why has the gorilla become so **endangered**?

• Loss of a home: As people build more homes and roads

There are few wild places left where a gorilla can find a home.

The mountain gorilla is close to extinction and is very rarely seen in the wild. Here, a baby mountain gorilla (*right*) eats while being held and protected by its mother.

and make use of the rain forest for farming, **logging,** and also mining, the gorilla is in danger of losing its home in the rain forest.
- **Bushmeat**: People who live in rain forest regions have always hunted wild animals to eat. In spite of laws to protect gorillas, many are still killed for sale as bushmeat.
- Trophies: The heads and hands of gorillas are prized among many Africans as trophies, and gorillas are trapped and killed so that body parts can be sold.
- Hunters have made money out of capturing wild gorillas for zoos.

A whole band of gorillas has been shot just to capture a single infant.

A BRIGHTER FUTURE?

In the African countries where gorillas are found, it is very hard to protect wildlife. Governments do not always value the rain forest and the animals that live there.

Enforcing laws that protect gorillas is critical. In addition, special tours to show gorillas in the wild can bring much-needed money to key African countries and help fund protected areas. Tours and other educational efforts may help save the gorilla and its rain forests.

Glossary

aggressive likely to attack

bachelor band a group of young males that have left the band where they were brought up but have not yet formed their own group with a harem of females

bands groups of gorillas that live together

canine teeth the longest, sharpest teeth, used for tearing food, fighting, and self-defense

cover trees, bushes or vegetation in which an animal can hide

endangered in danger of dying out in the wild

extinction when an animal has died out in the world

foraging searching for food

harem a group of females that are kept by one male for breeding

home range an area where a band of gorillas live

knuckle walking the way gorillas walk on their knuckles

logging the industry that cuts down trees to make paper, homes, furniture, and other wood products

mature fully grown

molar teeth flat teeth used for chewing and grinding

nutrients substances in food that are good for health and growth

parasites small insects, such as fleas or lice, that live on an animal

primate an order of mammals with a large brain and grasping hands and feet. It includes humans, apes, and monkeys.

rival one who competes with another

silverback a fully grown male gorilla

solitary living alone

species animals that are classified as a single, related group

threatening showing the intention of causing physical harm or injury

vegetarian an animal that eats only plants, such as fruit

vegetation a mass of plants

More Books to Read

The Gorilla. Endangered and Threatened Animals (series). Carl R. Green (Enslow)

Gorilla Doctors: Saving Endangered Great Apes. Scientists in the Field (series). Pamela S. Turner (Houghton Mifflin)

Gorillas. Animals, Animals (series). Judith Jango-Cohen (Benchmark Books)

Gorillas. Our Wild World (series). Deborah Dennard (Northwood Press)

Little Gorillas. Born to be Wild (series). Bernadette Costa-Prades (Gareth Stevens)

Web Sites

Gorilla Fun Facts
www.gorilla-haven.org/ghfunfacts.htm

Gorilla Foundation
koko.org/kidsclub/

Gorilla Watch
www.esa.int/esaKIDSen/SEMJXKXJD1E_Earth_0.html

Mountain Gorillas
www.iwrc-online.org/kids/Facts/Mammals/m_gorilla2.htm

National Geographic for Kids
www.nationalgeographic.com/kids/creature_feature/0007/gorillas.html

Publisher's note to educators and parents: Our editors have carefully reviewed these Web sites to ensure that they are suitable for children. Many Web sites change frequently, however, and we cannot guarantee that a site's future contents will continue to meet our high standards of quality and educational value. Be advised that children should be closely supervised whenever they access the Internet.

Index

African rain forests 4

baby gorillas 22, 24, 25, 26, 29
bands 6, 7, 11, 13, 14, 15, 16, 17, 18, 20, 21, 22, 23, 25, 26, 27, 29
breeding 7, 22, 23
bushmeat 29

crests 9

ears 10
eastern gorillas 5, 7, 14
enemies 5, 21, 28
extinction 28, 29
eyes 10

family groups 4, 5, 6, 8, 12, 13, 15, 27
feet 9
females 6, 7, 8, 9, 13, 15, 17, 18, 20, 21, 22, 23, 24, 27
fighting 4, 7, 8, 9, 18, 20, 21, 27
food 7, 9, 11, 12, 13, 14, 15, 21, 23, 25, 26, 27

grooming 14, 15, 21

hands 9, 18, 29
harems 7, 20, 22
heads 9, 19
hearing 10, 11
home ranges 6, 7, 17

knuckle walking 9

males 5, 6, 7, 8, 9, 14, 17, 19, 21, 22, 23, 26, 27
mountain gorillas 11, 13, 28, 29

nests 12, 15, 27
noseprints 11

playing 13, 14, 17, 27
pregnancy 24

resting 15

sign language 12, 28
silverbacks 6, 7, 8, 9, 13, 14, 15, 17, 18, 19, 20, 21, 22, 23, 25, 27
size 8, 9, 24
smell 11
sounds 16, 17

taste 11
teeth 9, 21
threat displays 18-19
touch 11
traveling 7, 15, 17, 25
twins 24

vegetarian 4, 7

western gorillas 5, 11, 14, 28